D0632196

The Witch of Endor
Copyright © 2008 by Gary Martin
Illustrations copyright © 2008 by Sergio Cariello

Requests for information should be addressed to:

Zondervan, *Grand Rapids, Michigan 49530*

CIP Applied for
ISBN: 978-0-310-71283-1

All Scripture quotations, unless otherwise indicated, are taken from the *Holy Bible: New International Version*®. NIV®. Copyright © 1973, 1978, 1984 by International Bible Society. Used by permission of Zondervan. All rights reserved.

All rights reserved. No part of this publication may be reproduced, stored in a retrieval system, or transmitted in any form or by any means—electronic, mechanical, photocopy, recording, or any other—except for brief quotations in printed reviews, without the prior permission of the publisher.

Internet addresses (websites, blogs, etc.) and telephone numbers printed in this book are offered as a resource to you. These are not intended in any way to be or imply an endorsement on the part of Zondervan, nor do we vouch for the content of these sites and numbers for the life of this book.

Series Editor: Bud Rogers
Managing Art Director: Merit Alderink

Printed in the United States of America

08 09 10 11 12 13 • 10 9 8 7 6 5 4 3 2 1

series editor: bud rogers

story by gary martin

art by sergio cariello

letters by dave lanphear

ZONDERVAN.com/
AUTHORTRACKER
follow your favorite authors

PROLOGUE
CIRCA 1440 B.C. THE NATION OF ISRAEL GROWS WEARY FROM THEIR CONTINUOUS WANDERING IN THE SINAI WILDERNESS.
SUFFERING HARDSHIP, THE ISRAELITES SOON FORGET THE MIRACLES GOD PERFORMED THROUGH MOSES THAT FREED THEM FROM THEIR SLAVERY IN EGYPT.
HAVE GOD AND MOSES BROUGHT US OUT OF EGYPT ONLY TO ACCOMPLISH OUR DEATH IN THIS WRETCHED WASTELAND?
WE DETEST THIS MISERABLE FOOD, AND WE HAVE NO WATER! IT WOULD BE BETTER FOR US TO HAVE DIED AS BONDSERVANTS IN EGYPT!

IN RESPONSE TO THE PEOPLE'S UNGRATEFULNESS, GOD SENDS COUNTLESS VENOMOUS SERPENTS.
THE SNAKES BITE THE PEOPLE AND MANY DIE.

THE ISRAELITES GO BEFORE MOSES AND REPENT.
WE SINNED WHEN WE SPOKE AGAINST THE LORD AND AGAINST YOU!
PLEASE INTERCEDE FOR US TO THE LORD, THAT HE MIGHT REMOVE THIS PLAGUE OF SERPENTS FROM AMONG US!

MOSES PRAYS FOR THE PEOPLE AND GOD TELLS HIM TO BUILD A BRONZE SERPENT AND SET IT UPON A STAFF...

...SO THAT ANYONE WHO IS BITTEN AND LOOKS UPON THE SERPENT STAFF* SHALL LIVE.
THE LORD BE PRAISED, WE ARE HEALED!
*THE STORY OF THE SERPENT STAFF CAN BE SEEN IN NUMBERS 21:4-9, 2 KINGS 18:1-4, AND JOHN 3:14-15

"THE HEAVY HAND OF GOD"
NEARLY 400 YEARS LATER, IN THE UNSAVORY TOWN OF LOD...

CURSE LORD AMALEK AND HIS LUST FOR GLORY! WE WERE LOYAL SOLDIERS FOR HIM, AND HE TOSSED US ASIDE LIKE SO MUCH RUBBISH!
AYE! NOW WE'RE REDUCED TO LURKING IN THE SHADOWS AND PREYING ON HAPLESS FOOLS!
THE HOUR OF DREAD DRAWS NEAR. WE'LL TARRY A MOMENT LONGER BEFORE WE WITHDRAW FOR THE NIGHT.
NOW HAND ME THE WINESKIN BEFORE YOU GLUG IT ALL DOWN!

AH! HERE COMES A PLUMP PIGEON!
WHILE I REFRESH MYSELF, YOU SHOULD REFLECT UPON YOUR RUDE BEHAVIOR...
...THEN I'LL ATTEND TO YOU SHORTLY.

BLESSINGS UPON THIS ESTABLISHMENT, GOOD INNKEEPER! IS IT POSSIBLE TO PURCHASE A MEAL AT THIS LATE HOUR?
YOU LOUT! SEE FOR YOURSELF, RIGHT OUTSIDE--PINK SNOW!
AYE, YOUNG SIR! I HAVE A FINE VENISON STEW SIMMERING ON THE HEARTH!
GERRAUGHH!
TAKE HEED! TWO THIEVING SCOUNDRELS ARE ACCOSTING YOUR CAMEL!
WORRY NOT. THE UNFORTUNATE KNAVES WILL LEARN THE MEANING OF REGRET WHEN UZAL INTRODUCES HIMSELF.

HAR HAR!
GOT YOU RIGHT IN THE--
ARGH!
SQUIRT

DETESTABLE CREATURE! I'LL REMOVE YOUR--
SQUIRT
DUCK!
THE BEAST'S SUPPLY OF CUD IS ENDLESS!
LEAVE THE CAMEL BE!
GRAB THE BUNDLES AND MAKE HASTE!

I TOLD YOU OUR PERSISTENCE WOULD PAY DIVIDENDS!
I GET FIRST CRACK AT THE UNDER-GARMENTS!
RUMBLE
UH-OH!

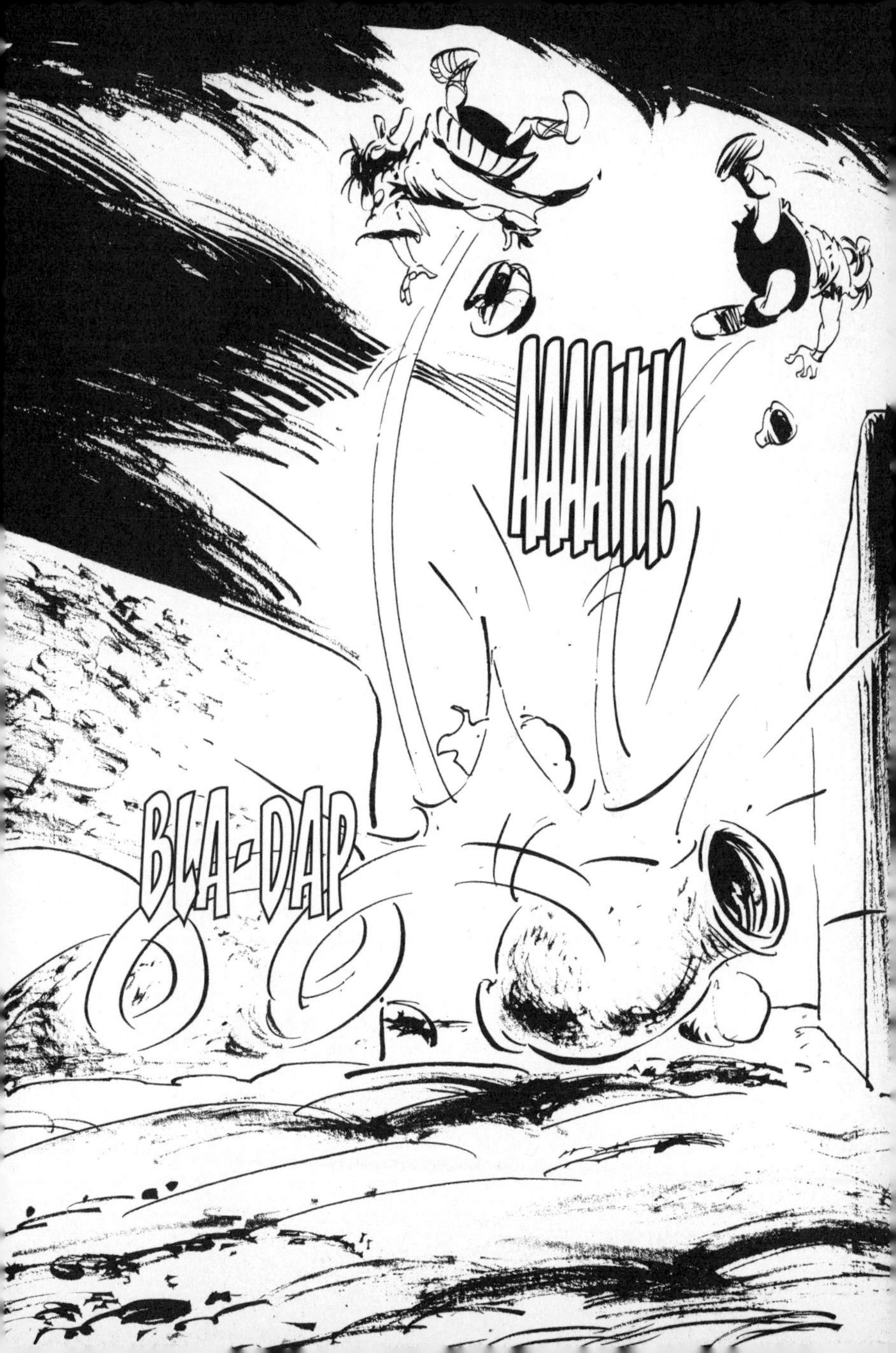
AAAAHH!
BLA-DAP

I'M IN NEED OF PRACTICE. MY TOSS FADED A BIT TO THE RIGHT.
DON'T STAND THERE GAWKING! RETRIEVE OUR GUEST'S BELONGINGS, WHILST I PREPARE HIM A HEARTY MEAL!

I HUMBLY APOLOGIZE FOR THE BEHAVIOR OF THOSE ROGUES. LOD WASN'T ALWAYS SO DISREPUTABLE.
I VISITED THIS TOWN IN MY YOUTH AND REMEMBER IT AS A THRIVING CENTER OF COMMERCE.
UH... GREETINGS
SO, WHAT WAS THE CAUSE OF LOD'S DOWNFALL?

LOD HAS HAD GOD'S HEAVY HAND UPON IT EVER SINCE THE GREAT LORD AMALEK RETURNED WITH THE SERPENT STAFF A MONTH AGO.
IT'S THE VERY STAFF MOSES HIMSELF FASHIONED FROM BRONZE TO HEAL THE ISRAELITES!
I KNOW YOU FROM SOMEWHERES.
WILL YOU LEAVE MY CUSTOMERS BE AND GO HOME TO YOUR WIFE?
YOUR FACE... I KNOW I'VE SEEN IT!

I THOUGHT THE SERPENT STAFF WAS KEPT INSIDE THE TABERNACLE AT SHILOH, ALONG WITH THE OTHER HOLY ARTIFACTS OF THE HEBREW NATION.

APPARENTLY, THE STAFF WAS REMOVED FROM THE TEMPLE BY THE ISRAELITE PRIESTS AND USED TO BOLSTER THE FAITH OF THE HEBREWS IN NEARBY CITIES.
WHEN AMALEK HEARD THE STAFF WAS ON TOUR, HE AND HIS ELITE GUARDS SNATCHED IT FROM THE PRIESTS AND THEIR SENTRIES. LORD AMALEK IS A MIGHTY WARRIOR, AND HIS FEATS IN BATTLE ARE LEGENDARY.

"ON ONE OCCASION, LORD AMALEK LED A HUNDRED SOLDIERS TO THE NORTHERN TERRITORY TO INVESTIGATE A REPORT OF INVADING TROOPS.
"TO HIS SURPRISE, THE PHILISTINE LORD AND HIS SMALL CADRE ENCOUNTERED A VAST BABYLONIAN ARMY!

"HOPELESSLY OUTNUMBERED...
"...AMALEK'S SOLDIERS WERE INEVITABLY WHITTLED DOWN...
"...UNTIL ONLY AMALEK AND HIS PERSONAL GUARDS, THE THREE WARRIOR MAIDENS OF GOSHEN, HAD SURVIVED.

"THE BABYLONIAN COMMANDER PLEADED FOR THE REMAINING FOUR TO SURRENDER...
"...BUT AMALEK AND HIS FIERCE MAIDENS REFUSED...
"...AND THE BABYLONIANS ATTACKED IN A MASSIVE HORDE!

"THE BATTLE RAGED...
"...AND REMARKABLY...
"...WHEN THE DUST SETTLED, AMALEK AND HIS WARRIOR MAIDENS REMAINED STANDING AMONG A MULTITUDE OF FALLEN ATTACKERS!

"CUTTING HIS LOSSES, THE BABYLONIAN COMMANDER RETREATED WITH WHAT REMAINED OF HIS ARMY."
ALAS, THOSE WERE THE DAYS OF GLORY FOR AMALEK.
NOW HE HOLES UP IN HIS CITADEL WITH HIS PRECIOUS SERPENT STAFF, WHILE THE CITIZENS OF LOD SUFFER OPPRESSION FROM THE HEBREW GOD.
AH-HA! I KNOW YOU! YOU'RE THE ONE WHO HEFTED THE GAZA GATE IN HEBRON!
YOU'RE THE SON OF SAMSON!

TREMENDOUS! WE'RE HONORED TO SERVE THE SON OF THE MIGHTY SAMSON!
JUST IMAGINE IF YOU AND LORD AMALEK COULD MEET IN BATTLE!
THAT'S A SPECTACLE I WOULD SURELY PAY TO SEE!

MUMBLE MUMBLE
CLOSING TIME!
YOU BELIEVE ME, DON'T YOU... PINK SNOW!
SURE, SURE. NOW SCAMPER ON HOME.

WHERE ARE MY MANNERS? YOU MUST BE WEARY FROM YOUR TRAVELS.
I INSIST YOU STAY THE NIGHT AS MY GUEST.
YOU HAVE MY THANKS!

HERE IS YOUR ROOM. IT'S MY FINEST ACCOMMODATION.
MAY I ASK THE PURPOSE OF THE FOOD BASKET?
YOUR CAMEL WILL BE WELL ATTENDED BY MY SERVANT. HAVE A PLEASANT SLEEP.

LATER THAT NIGHT...
AIIIEEE!
HUH?
THAT CAME FROM OUTSIDE!
WHAT...?

GOD IN HEAVEN!

BE THEY APPARITIONS OR FLESH AND BLOOD-- I'LL NOT REST...
...UNTIL I UNRAVEL THESE STRANGE GOINGS-ON!

GERRR!

BA-WAM
KRASH

GONE?!?

THE NEXT MORNING...
UZAL, WE'LL GET BREAKFAST DOWN THE ROAD. I CAN'T WAIT TO SHAKE THE DUST OFF MY FEET FROM THIS BIZARRE TOWN!
ONE MOMENT, PLEASE.
WE REPRESENT THE MUNICIPAL TRANSPORTATION GUILD. YOU OWE A TEN-SHEKEL FREIGHT TAX FOR HAULING THIS CARGO THROUGH TOWN.

WITH *RESPECT,* GENTLEMEN, YOU DON'T *LOOK--* UM--*MAY* I SEE YOUR *CREDENTIALS?*
THIS IS MY CREDENTIAL!

BE WARNED! I DO NOT ENVY YOUR ACHING HEADS IF YOU PERSIST WITH THIS FOOLISHNESS!
SEIZE HIM!

AAAAAH!
UHH!

ARE YOU LODITES ALL DERANGED?
A STRANGER ENTERS YOUR TOWN AND YOU LICK YOUR JOWLS LIKE RAVENOUS JACKALS!
BUT AS YOU'RE ABOUT TO SEE...
...I AM NO HELPLESS LAMB!
CEASE!

PLEASE, YOUNG MASTER, DO NOT STRIKE MY BROTHER! WE RESPECTFULLY BEG YOUR FORGIVENESS!
THIS CONFRONTATION WAS MERELY A TEST!

OUR THANKS FOR YOUR INDULGENCE AND FOR GIVING EAR TO OUR PROPOSAL.
I AM AZIZA, AND THIS IS MY BROTHER, JAREB. WE DESPERATELY NEED THE HELP OF SAMSON'S SON.
AS YOU HAVE SEEN, LOD IS UNDER A DARK CLOUD, AND ITS PEOPLE ARE SUFFERING!
WE WANT THE SERPENT STAFF OF MOSES RETURNED TO SHILOH SO LOD CAN BE SPARED FROM THE WRATH OF THE HEBREW GOD!
THIS TOWN IS UNDER A DOUBLE CURSE.
AFTER LORD AMALEK ATTAINED THE STAFF, HE SECLUDED HIMSELF WITHIN HIS CITADEL. NOW HIS MAIN RIVAL IS UNFETTERED TO PURSUE HER BLACK SCHEMES!

"SHE IS THE POWERFUL SORCERESS FROM ENDOR, AND SHE SEEKS TO POSSESS THE SACRED SERPENT STAFF AND ITS GIFT OF LIFE ETERNAL!"

SINCE AMALEK'S SOLDIERS ARE NOW UNEMPLOYED, THE WITCH'S NOCTURNAL MINIONS ARE UNRESTRAINED TO ROAM LOD'S STREETS.
I HAD AN INTIMATE ENCOUNTER WITH ONE OF THOSE CREATURES LAST NIGHT.
THE TOWN'S FOLK SET OUT FOOD, HOPING THE FIENDS WON'T INVADE THEIR HOMES.
I ONCE SERVED IN AMALEK'S CITADEL, AND I KNOW WHERE THE STAFF IS LOCATED. BUT WE NEED YOUR MIGHT TO OVERCOME THE CITADEL'S FORMIDABLE DEFENSES.

I'D LIKE TO SURVEY AMALEK'S FORTRESS BEFORE I MAKE A DECISION.
I THANK YOU FOR THE PEOPLE OF LOD, AND FOR EVEN CONSIDERING TO LEND YOUR AID.
AHEM! MAY I SUGGEST WE SCOUT THE CITADEL AFTER DARK WHILE THE STREETS ARE DESERTED? WE'LL REMAIN SAFE IF WE RETURN BEFORE THE CREATURES EMERGE.

LATE THAT NIGHT, ON THE OUTSKIRTS OF LORD AMALEK'S CITADEL...
THE TERRACE ON THE TOWER'S CREST IS AMALEK'S PRIVATE QUARTERS.
CAN WE SCALE IT?
THE WALLS ARE UNCLIMBABLE. WE'LL HAVE TO ASCEND FROM WITHIN.
THE SENTRY'S BARRACKS ARE LOCATED ON THE GROUND FLOOR. AMALEK RETAINED HIS BEST SOLDIERS TO GUARD THE TOWER'S COURTYARD.

THAT FIERCE BELLOW IS COMING FROM ONE OF THE LEVELS IN THE CENTER OF THE TOWER. AMALEK HAS UNKNOWN DEFENSES THAT RESIDE BELOW HIS RESIDENCE.
I'D LIKE MORE INFORMATION FROM YOUR SISTER ABOUT THE TOWER'S INTERIOR.
ROARRR

GERR-RIND
IT'S TIME WE DEPART. THE NIGHT CREATURES ARE EMERGING FROM THEIR LAIR!

A FEW MINUTES LATER, AT JAREB'S HOME...
MASTER JAREB! YOUR SISTER'S BEEN ABDUCTED!
I HEARD A SCREAM, AND I WENT INTO AZIZA'S ROOM AND SAW NIGHT FIENDS PULLING HER THROUGH THE WINDOW!

DAGON, NO!

I SHOULD HAVE FORESEEN THIS!
THAT VILE WITCH SEIZED MY DEAR SISTER BECAUSE AZIZA WORKED AT THE CITADEL AND KNOWS ITS SECRETS!
DON'T LOSE HEART. WE'LL FOLLOW THE CREATURES TO THEIR DOMAIN AND RETURN AZIZA TO SAFETY!
IT'S HOPELESS! THE CREATURES DWELL DEEP WITHIN ANCIENT CATACOMBS UNDER THE CITY!
THEN GET TO YOUR FEET AND FETCH SOME TORCHES!

CHAPTER 2
"ASHTORETH OFFERING"
WHAT VILE CREATURES DWELL WITHIN THE EARTH'S PITCH-BLACK BOWELS?
JAREB, SINCE SHE'S YOUR SISTER, YOU GO FIRST!
OH NO! THAT'S WHY I HIRED THESE ARMED RUFFIANS.

UHH... WE THOUGHT THE DESCENDANT OF SAMSON WAS LEADING US!

LET'S TEST ITS DEPTH.
PLINK
I ESTIMATE ABOUT FOURTEEN CUBITS.
AS I DESCEND INTO THE PITS OF SHEOL, THE LORD GOD IS WITH ME!

TOSS ME THE TORCH!

IN THIS DARKNESS, I ADVISE WE STAY CLOSE TOGETHER.
THESE CAVERNS ARE VAST! WHICH DIRECTION SHOULD WE GO?
EASTERLY WILL TAKE US UNDER THE HEART OF THE CITY.
GRUNT!

SOMETHING'S BACK THERE!
WE NEED TO PICK UP OUR PACE!
ZADOK! IF YOU STEP ON MY FOOT ONCE MORE...!
WHAT'S THE SOURCE OF THIS DRIPPING WATER?
THE TUNNEL MUST BE NEAR THE UNDERGROUND SPRING THAT SUPPLIES THE CITY WITH WATER.

AAAHH!
ZADOK?
WHERE'S ZADOK?!?
HE'S GONE, TANIS. FORGET HIM.

WHAT DO YOU MEAN, FORGET HIM? HE'S OUR COMRADE!
OUR PAYMENT IS TOO MEAGER FOR THIS! WE SHOULD ABANDON THIS SEARCH AND TURN BACK!
FINE, SAMADIN! THE EXIT'S THAT WAY!
FOLLOW ME OR RETURN TO THE SURFACE.
WISE CHOICE.

CARVINGS OF ANCIENT DEITIES! COULD THIS BE SOME FORGOTTEN TEMPLE?
NOT FORGOTTEN. THIS MUST BE THE UNDERGROUND SHRINE OF THE GODDESS ASHTORETH. IT'S RUMORED THAT HER ZEALOTS STILL PERFORM HUMAN SACRIFICES HERE!

STRANGE...

WHAT MANNER OF BLACK LIQUID POOLS AT OUR FEET?
OVER HERE!

AZIZA!

PRAISE TO DAGON, MY SISTER YET LIVES!
SHE'S MERELY UNCONSCIOUS. TAKE HER WHILE I FETCH SOME WATER.
MAKE HASTE! SOMETHING APPROACHES IN THE DARKNESS!

SHE'S AWAKENING!
BRANAN! I PRAYED YOU'D COME FOR ME!
WELL... UM...
...HERE. JAREB, TAKE YOUR SISTER.
AZIZA, IT'S BEST YOU STAND NOW. WE NEED BRANAN'S STRONG ARMS PUT TO BETTER USE!

THEY BLOCK OUR PASSAGE! IS THERE ANOTHER WAY OUT?
IF THERE IS, IT'S UNKNOWN TO ME!

HOLD FAST! LET THEM BRING THE FIGHT TO US!
THEY HESITATE. WHY DON'T THEY ATTACK?
GRUNT!
HUH?

GER-ARR!

WACK
URK...
AAAH...
SAMADIN!

STAND TIGHTLY TOGETHER AND DON'T STRAY FROM THE TORCH!
THESE CAVE DWELLERS DETEST THE LIGHT!
WHA--?
UNHAND ME, BRUTE!

ARG!
BRANAN...
...NOOO!

I SAID, UNHAND ME!
BE YOU MAN OR BEAST...
...YOU'LL NOT SEIZE ME AGAIN!
OH LORD, GIVE ME SIGHT INTO THIS DARKNESS THAT I MIGHT SEND MY ENEMIES...

...BACK TO SHEOL!
THA-BOW

KA-BASH

STILL *HUNGER* FOR THE *TASTE* OF MY *MALLET?*
APPARENTLY NOT.

GET BACK, FIENDS!

BLAA-DOW

ARE YOU...?
FINE, THANKS TO YOU!
AND TANIS?
NOT SO FORTUNATE.
THE DRIPPING WATER IS DOUSING THE TORCH, AND THE CREATURES GROW BOLDER!

GERRRR!
GER-ARR!

GRUNT!

BACK!
SPL ASH
FA-FOOM

ARRRGH!

TIME TO--COFF-- DEPART!
I-- HACK-- AGREE!

BLOCKED!
THE CAVERN'S ENGULFED! WHAT NOW!?!

GRUNT!
THACK

THA-WAK

WHA-WOOOOSH

HOLD ON!

AFTER THAT... SIMPLE ERRAND...FETCHING THE SERPENT STAFF...SHOULD BE A TRIFLE.

CHAPTER 3 "THE WITCH AND THE WARRIOR"
THE NEXT DAY, INSIDE THE RESIDENCE OF JAREB AND AZIZA...
INDEED. FOR IT'S MUCH SMALLER THAN THE GAZA GATE YOU HEFTED IN HEBRON.*
*SEE THIS FEAT IN VOLUME 1, THE JUDGE OF GOD.

FOR TONIGHT'S ASSAULT ON AMALEK'S STRONGHOLD, OUR FIRST OBSTACLE IS THE CITADEL'S LARGE CEDAR GATE. IT'S HEAVILY BARRED FROM INSIDE.
BUT FOR THE MIGHTY SON OF SAMSON, IT SHOULD POSE NO PROBLEM.

WHEN THE GATE IS TOPPLED, THE COURTYARD SENTRIES WILL RESPOND QUICKLY.
JAREB AND HIS BAND OF MERCENARIES WILL ENGAGE THE GUARDS WHILE YOU PROCEED THROUGH THE BARRACKS AND ASCEND THE STAIRS TO THE SECOND LEVEL.
ARE JAREB'S MEN RELIABLE?
THEY'RE ALL SEASONED SOLDIERS AND HIGHLY MOTIVATED, BECAUSE THEY SERVED IN AMALEK'S ARMY BUT WERE PROMPTLY DISCHARGED WHEN HE ACQUIRED THE SERPENT STAFF.
I GO NOW TO PREPARE MY MEN. WE'LL MEET AFTER SUNSET AT THE CITADEL GATE.

WHAT WILL I ENCOUNTER ON THE SECOND LEVEL?
A FEARSOME BLACK BEAST THAT WILL RATTLE YOUR BONES WITH ITS BELLOWING ROAR!
THE THIRD LEVEL HOUSES AMALEK'S THREE ELITE SENTINELS, THE WARRIOR MAIDENS OF GOSHEN! DO NOT BE MISLED BY THEIR FEMALE GENDER. THEIR FEROCITY IN BATTLE IS UNEQUALED.
THE TOP LEVEL IS THE RESIDENCE OF LORD AMALEK HIMSELF. IT POSES THE GREATEST DANGER.
THE SERPENT STAFF IS KEPT ON AN ALTAR IN AMALEK'S SLEEPING QUARTERS. TAKE HEED, AMALEK'S PROWESS IN COMBAT CANNOT BE UNDERSTATED.
THE HOST HE'S SENT TO THE AFTERLIFE IS COUNTLESS!

YOU SHOULD REPLENISH YOUR STRENGTH BEFORE TONIGHT'S ASSAULT.
I'LL FETCH SOME FOOD. THEN YOU MUST REST.
MASTER, MAY I REMOVE YOUR SANDALS SO YOU CAN RELAX IN COMFORT?
THAT'S A GRACIOUS OFFER, BUT I CAN DO IT MYSELF.
IT IS MY PLEASURE TO SERVE THE SON OF THE CHOSEN NAZIRITE TO THE ALMIGHTY GOD!
YOU KNOW OF MY FATHER?
WELL ENOUGH TO KNOW HE WAS EASILY DECEIVED BY THE ENCHANTING SMILE OF A SCHEMING WOMAN.

YOU APPEAR YOUNGER THAN ME. HOW IS IT YOU KNEW...?
WHOM ARE YOU CONVERSING WITH?
YOUR YOUNG SERVANT.
YOUR FATIGUE MUST BE GREATER THAN I IMAGINED.
I HAVE NO YOUNG SERVANT!

LATER THAT NIGHT...
QUICKLY RUSH INTO THE COURTYARD AFTER THE GATE FALLS AND ENGAGE THE SENTRIES BEFORE THEY CAN ASSEMBLE IN MASS.

HEH, HEH--HOO-BOY!
I APOLOGIZE. WHO COULD HAVE IMAGINED THE SON OF SAMSON ALLYING HIMSELF WITH PHILISTINE SOLDIERS?!
HUMM... YOU TWO LOOK FAMILIAR.
NO, NO! WE'VE NOT MET!
NO, NEVER!

TIME IS WASTING! PLEASE PROCEED!
CREEEK
DRAW YOUR WEAPONS AND PREPARE FOR GLORY!

UH...
WHAT'S
HE--?

AMEN.

I'LL TRADE THIS DELICIOUS TURNIP FOR YOUR DRIED-UP GRAPES.
HA! I SCOFF AT YOUR PUNY TURNIP. THESE GRAPES ARE SWEET AND JUICY!
HEY! YOU CHILDREN! CLIMB DOWN FROM THERE!
MUNCH
GOBBLE
CHILDREN?

HEY!
CRASH
BASH
?

KER-SMASH
SOUND THE ALARM! WE'RE UNDER ATTACK!

KRASH
KRUNCH
KLANG

BLAP
AAH!

THONK

ZZZZZZZ!
GRRRR!

GER-ROARRR!

CLANG
SWOOOSH

BA-WHAM

GREETINGS, YOUNG WARRIOR!
AND A MOST HANDSOME WARRIOR AT THAT!

YOU MUST BE MIGHTY INDEED TO GET PAST OUR PET!
SMASH
SWOOSH
THAK

UNNHHH!
CHUNK
SWORD STUCK?

HALT!
WOULD YOU DARE LAY A HAND ON A HELPLESS GIRL?
KRAK

THUMP
AIIEEEE!
BOINK
SLICE
SLICE

OUCH!
TRIP

KA-BAMM

YOU MIGHT NOT APPRECIATE THIS...
RRRRRIP
...BUT THERE'S A SOUND I ALWAYS FIND AMUSING.
LISTEN CLOSELY NOW!

IT'S TWO HEAD BONES THUMPING TOGETHER!
CLONK
IT SOUNDS LIKE COCONUTS!
FLOP
IT WORKS EVERY TIME!

AMALEK! STEP OUT AND FACE ME!
AMALEK?
THE ALTAR!

THE SERPENT STAFF OF MOSES!

COFF!
COFF! COFF!
WHO ARE YOU, AND WHERE IS AMALEK?

THE SHELL YOU SEE BEFORE YOU WAS ONCE THE GREAT LORD AMALEK!
COFF!-COFF!
NOW MY FRAIL BODY CARRIES THE JUST PENALTY OF MY CRIMES AGAINST THE GOD OF ISRAEL.
IT'S TOO LATE FOR ME...
COFF!
...TO BE SPARED HIS WRATH. BUT THE PEOPLE OF LOD CAN YET BE SAVED!
CARRY THE STAFF FAR AWAY FROM HERE.

I WILL RETURN THE SERPENT STAFF TO THE HEBREW TABERNACLE.
THIS I VOW!
Branan!
Branan, my son!
It is I-- SAMSON!

I have come from the grave to warn you, my son! Amalek is evil and not to be trusted.
Amalek should be killed to protect the innocent from his sinful schemes.
SOMETHING IS AMISS! WHY WOULD GOD WANT ME TO SLAY A DYING MAN?

Amalek is evil and must be killed! Aziza has been chosen to return the serpent staff!
Obey me, my son! Kill Amalek!
THIS SEEMS WRONG, AND NOT AT ALL OF GOD'S CHARACTER!

I HAVE IT!
WHAT'S THIS?
AT LONG LAST, THE STAFF!

ALL PRAISE TO THE GODDESS ASHTORETH!
THANK YOU FOR DELIVERING UNTO YOUR HUMBLE SERVANT THE SACRED SERPENT STAFF OF MOSES AND FULFILLING MY QUEST FOR IMMORTALITY!

KRACKA-

-DOOM

KOFF!
WHAT...?
AZIZA!
JAREB!
THE SMOKE IS BLINDING!

NO WAY OUT!
WELL, HERE GOES ...

THE STAFF!

CRASHHH

munch
munch

A FEW DAYS LATER...
YOUNG BRANAN, WAIT!
SOMETHING TO GNAW ON DURING YOUR JOURNEY.
YOUR GENEROSITY OVERWHELMS ME!
WE HAVE PLENTY NOW SINCE THE NIGHT FIENDS NO LONGER RETURN.
AND THE TOWN IS THRIVING BECAUSE YOU ARE RETURNING THE MAGICAL STAFF TO THE HEBREW TEMPLE!

DO NOT MAKE THE SAME ASSUMPTION ABOUT THE SERPENT STAFF AS SOME HAVE MADE TOWARD SAMSON'S FAMOUS HAIR.
THESE THINGS POSSESS NO POWER OF THEIR OWN. BUT RATHER, THE POWER COMES FROM THE CREATOR; THE VERY LIVING GOD HIMSELF!
FAREWELL!
THE END
BRANAN'S ADVENTURES CONTINUE IN BOOK 6: THE HEROES OF GOD

GREETINGS, LOYAL READERS! I ADMIT YOUR MODERN COMMUNICATION IS BEYOND MY UNDERSTANDING.
THREE THOUSAND YEARS AGO, IF I WANTED TO SEND A LETTER TO A FRIEND IN A DISTANT TOWN, I'D HAVE TO CARVE MY WRITING ON A CLAY TABLET AND CARRY IT BY CARAVAN TO ITS DESTINATION.
YOU GOOD FOLKS HAVE A WONDERMENT CALLED EMAIL! I'D LOVE TO HEAR FROM YOU, SO PLEASE SEND YOUR COMMENTS TO ZREVIEW@ZONDERVAN.COM. OR IF YOU LIKE, YOU CAN ALWAYS SEND IT MY WAY BY THE NEXT PASSING CAMEL!
BRANAN WANTS YOU!
SEND YOUR COMMENTS ON
SON OF SAMSON TO
ZREVIEW@ZONDERVAN.COM

BRANAN
STANDING SIX FEET TWO INCHES AND WEIGHING TWO HUNDRED AND FORTY POUNDS, THE EIGHTEEN-YEAR-OLD SON OF SAMSON HAS INHERITED HIS FATHER'S INCREDIBLE STRENGTH. RAISED BY HIS PHILISTINE MOTHER, BRANAN GREW UP IN THE TOWN OF GATH. HE NOW TRAVELS THE ANCIENT LANDS OF PALESTINE, RETRACING THE LEGENDARY DEEDS OF THE FATHER HE NEVER KNEW.

AZIZA
ONCE A SERVANT IN LORD AMALEK'S CITADEL, THE BEAUTEOUS AZIZA (ALONG WITH HER BROTHER JAREB) SEEKS THE AID OF SAMSON'S SON TO RECOVER THE FABLED SERPENT STAFF OF MOSES AND RETURN IT TO THE TABERNACLE OF THE GOD OF ISRAEL. AZIZA'S INTENTIONS SEEM HONORABLE, BUT THERE APPEARS TO BE MUCH MORE TO THIS PLUCKY SERVANT GIRL THAN MEETS THE EYE.

LORD AMALEK

NUMEROUS INCREDIBLE TALES ARE ATTRIBUTED TO THIS POWERFUL PHILISTINE LORD AND HIS LEGENDARY FEATS OF COMBAT. EXAGGERATED OR NOT, AMALEK'S REPUTATION AS A DYNAMIC AND FIERCE WARRIOR HAS RIGHTFULLY GAINED HIM BOTH FEAR AND RESPECT FROM HEBREWS AND PHILISTINES ALIKE. THE SON OF SAMSON HAS ENCOUNTERED MANY INTIMIDATING FOES ON THE BATTLEFIELD, BUT HE HAS YET TO FACE THE LIKES OF THE MIGHTY LORD AMALEK!

THREE WARRIOR MAIDENS OF GOSHEN
FIERCELY LOYAL TO LORD AMALEK, IT IS UNKNOWN HOW THESE THREE WARRIOR MAIDENS ACQUIRED THEIR PROFICIENCY IN COMBAT. DO NOT BE FOOLED BY THE ALLURING CHARMS OF THESE EGYPTIAN BEAUTIES. WITH TWINKLING EYES AND FLATTERING TONGUES, THEY WILL BEGUILE YOUR SENSES BEFORE A FLASH OF THEIR BLADES SENDS YOU TO YOUR MAKER.

SAMSON
SAMSON WAS GREATLY EMPOWERED BY GOD WITH AWESOME STRENGTH, YET HE FAILED TO FULLY UTILIZE HIS EXTRAORDINARY GIFTS FOR GOD'S GLORY. SAMSON WAS A JUDGE OF ISRAEL FOR TWENTY YEARS. THE SON OF SAMSON UNDERTAKES HIS JOURNEY OF DISCOVERY (APPROXIMATELY) TEN YEARS AFTER SAMSON'S HEROIC DEATH. (THE EXPLOITS OF SAMSON ARE CHRONICLED IN THE BOOK OF JUDGES, CHAPTERS 13-16.)

GROWING UP IN SAN JOSE, CALIFORNIA, GARY MARTIN'S DREAM WAS TO BECOME A COMIC BOOK ARTIST. AT AGE 24, HE PACKED UP HIS DRAWING BOARD AND MOVED TO NEW YORK CITY, HOME OF MARVEL AND DC COMICS. LIFE IN NEW YORK WAS NEVER DULL FOR THE CALIFORNIA BOY. EVEN A MUNDANE COMMUTE BY SUBWAY INTO MANHATTAN COULD TURN INTO AN ENTERTAINING RENDITION OF THE JETSONS THEME SONG BY AN ECCENTRIC PASSENGER. AFTER GARY'S SIX-YEAR STINT AS A STARVING ARTIST (LITERALLY), HE LANDED A REGULAR GIG AS AN INKER, AND WAS ABLE TO SAY GOOD-BYE TO THE BIG APPLE.

IN 1986, GARY MOVED BACK TO THE WEST COAST, AND HAS BEEN A FREELANCE COMIC BOOK ARTIST AND WRITER EVER SINCE. HE'S WORKED FOR ALL THE MAJOR COMPANIES, INCLUDING MARVEL, DC, DARK HORSE, IMAGE, AND DISNEY, AND ON SUCH TITLES AS, SPIDER-MAN, X-MEN, BATMAN, STAR WARS, AND MICKEY MOUSE. GARY IS BEST KNOWN FOR HIS POPULAR HOW-TO BOOKS ENTITLED THE ART OF COMIC BOOK INKING. RECENTLY, GARY WROTE A COMIC BOOK SERIES CALLED THE MOTH, WHICH HE CO-CREATED WITH ARTIST STEVE RUDE. GARY'S HAPPY DAYS ARE NOW SPENT INKING AT HOME (IN HIS PJS AND FUZZY SLIPPERS), WRITING SON OF SAMSON STORIES AND TRYING TO TEACH HIS LOVELY BRAZILIAN WIFE, MARIA, THE THEME SONG TO THE JETSONS.

SERGIO CARIELLO WAS BORN IN 1964. HE BEGAN HIS CAREER AT THE AGE OF ELEVEN, WRITING, DRAWING, AND LETTERING HIS OWN COMIC STRIP, FREDERICO, THE DETECTIVE, FOR A LOCAL NEWSPAPER IN BRAZIL WHERE HE ALSO DREW POLITICAL CARICATURES UNTIL THE AGE OF FOURTEEN. HE DREAMED OF ONE DAY BECOMING A COMIC BOOK ARTIST IN THE UNITED STATES. HE PAID HIS TUITION FOR LEARNING ENGLISH AS A SECOND LANGUAGE WITH DRAWINGS USED IN THEIR LECTURING BOOKS. HE MIGRATED TO THE USA IN 1985. IN 1986, HE ENROLLED AS A STUDENT AT THE WORD OF LIFE BIBLE INSTITUTE IN UPSTATE NEW YORK, WHERE HE ALSO PAID SOME OF HIS TUITION FEES WITH DRAWINGS AND CARICATURES.

IN 1987, HE ATTENDED THE JOE KUBERT SCHOOL OF CARTOONS AND GRAPHIC ARTS IN NEW JERSEY. HE WORKED ON HIS FIRST AMERICAN COMIC BOOK, DAGON, FOR CALIBER PRESS, WHILE STILL A STUDENT AT THE KUBERT SCHOOL. DURING HIS SECOND SCHOOL YEAR, HE WAS HIRED TO LETTER BOOKS FOR MARVEL COMICS, AND HE WAS QUICKLY MOVED ON TO DRAW SOME OF THEIR MAIN CHARACTERS SUCH AS SPIDER-MAN, DAREDEVIL, AND THE AVENGERS. HE ALSO ILLUSTRATED MANY OF DC COMICS' CHARACTERS LIKE SUPERMAN, DEATHSTROKE, WONDER WOMAN, THE FLASH, AZRAEL AND BATMAN.

IN 1997, SERGIO REJOINED THE JOE KUBERT SCHOOL TO TEACH FOR SEVEN CONSECUTIVE YEARS, CONTRIBUTING TO PRODUCE MANY OF TODAY'S LEADING CARTOONISTS. HE LATER BECAME THE FIRST TO HELP JOE KUBERT AS AN INSTRUCTOR FOR THE SCHOOL'S CORRESPONDENCE COURSES. DURING THIS PERIOD, HE ALSO WORKED FOR VARIOUS PUBLISHERS, INCLUDING DRAWING A MONTHLY TITLE FOR DC COMICS.

IN 2005, SERGIO JOINED FORCES WITH ACCLAIMED WRITER CHUCK DIXON TO LAUNCH HIS FIRST CO-CREATOR-OWNED PROPERTY, THE IRON GHOST, A MINISERIES PUBLISHED BY IMAGE AND ATP COMICS. SERGIO ALSO WON FIRST PRIZE IN THE FIRST INTERNATIONAL CHRISTIAN COMICS COMPETITION FOR NO PROFIT! (A TWO-PAGE COMIC BASED ON ECCLESIASTES 5). THAT YEAR, SERGIO ALSO ILLUSTRATED AND DONATED SEVERAL PAGES TO TEMPEST, THE HURRICANE KATRINA RELIEF PROJECT PUT TOGETHER BY COMMUNITY COMICS, WHICH LED TO THE PROJECT YOU NOW HOLD IN YOUR HANDS!

SERGIO IS ALSO KNOWN FOR HIS RUN IN THE LONE RANGER SERIES FOR DYNAMITE ENTERTAINMENT, CRUX FOR CROSSGEN COMICS, THE SAINTS FOR LAYNE MORGAN MEDIA, AS WELL AS MANY OTHER PROJECTS ABROAD.

SERGIO CARIELLO AND HIS WIFE, LUZIA, LIVE IN SUNNY FLORIDA WITH THEIR ADORABLE DOG, A WEST HIGHLANDER WHITE TERRIER, CALLED MONIQUE. THEY WORSHIP WITH THE BODY OF SAINTS UNDER PASTOR JOE CERRETA, WHERE THEY SERVE AS DIRECTOR OF THE CONTEMPORARY PRAISE AND WORSHIP TEAM AND KIDS' MINISTRIES, RESPECTIVELY.

LEARN MORE ABOUT SERGIO CARIELLO BY VISITING WWW.SERGIOCARIELLO.NET

SON OF SAMSON'S *LETTERER, DAVE LANPHEAR, HEADS ARTMONKEYS STUDIOS. YOU CAN FIND THEIR WORK TODAY AT MANY PUBLISHERS, INCLUDING MARVEL, DC'S CMX, DISNEY, DARK HORSE, URBAN MINISTRIES, NACHSHON PRESS AND, VERY PROUDLY, HERE FOR ZONDERVAN.*

IT'S ESTIMATED DAVE'S LETTERED OVER 40,000 COMIC BOOK PAGES, ENOUGH TO TILE THE LARGEST COMIC BOOK CONVENTION'S FLOOR FOUR TIMES. HE'S WORKED IN THREE MAJOR STUDIOS: MALIBU COMICS, COMICRAFT, AND CROSSGEN COMICS AT THEIR MOST PROLIFIC TIMES. HE'S BEEN BLESSED TO WORK WITH TALENTED WRITERS, ARTISTS AND EDITORS, COUNTING MANY AS FRIENDS, AND HAS HAD THE PRIVILEGE TO WORK ON NUMEROUS PRESTIGIOUS PROJECTS SINCE THE 1990S. HE HAS ALSO RECEIVED SEVERAL AWARDS FOR HIS LETTERING.

DAVE IS A THREE-TIME EDITORIAL CARTOON WINNER, AND HAS ALSO BEEN A CARICATURIST, COMIC STRIP CARTOONIST, NEWSPAPER ILLUSTRATOR, STORYBOARD ARTIST (NOTABLY ON PBS' DRAGON TALES), MAGAZINE DESIGNER, TALENT COORDINATOR, AND PUBLISHING CONSULTANT. BUT ABOVE ALL THOSE POSITIONS, DAVE LIKES HIS CURRENT WORK BEST: HUSBAND TO HIS BEAUTIFUL WIFE NATALIE, AND STAY-AT-HOME DAD TO THEIR THREE SONS.

*COME READ **BEHIND THE LINES,** THE ARTMONKEYS BLOG AT HTTP://ARTMONKEYS.BLOGSPOT.COM, OR SEE THEIR GALLERY AT WWW.ARTMONKEYS.WEEBLY.COM.*

BUD ROGERS IS A CARTOONIST AND AN EDITOR OF INSPIRATIONAL COMICS AND GRAPHIC NOVELS. HE HAS BEEN VERY ACTIVE IN THE CHRISTIAN COMICS COMMUNITY, SERVING FOR MANY YEARS ON THE BOARD OF DIRECTORS FOR THE CHRISTIAN COMICS ARTS SOCIETY AND PROVIDING ENCOURAGEMENT, SUPPORT, AND GUIDANCE TO WRITERS AND ARTISTS.
IN 2003, HE HELPED FORM COMMUNITY COMICS, A VIRTUAL STUDIO, PRODUCTION HOUSE, AND INDEPENDENT PUBLISHER. WITHIN COMMUNITY COMICS, HE HELPED BRING SEVERAL PROJECTS TO FRUITION FROM THE VERY BEGINNING OF AN IDEA TO FINAL PUBLISHED FORM.
WHEN BUD'S NOT EDITING OR WORKING ON HIS OWN CARTOONS, HE ENJOYS MUSIC, COOKING, AND CATCHING THE OCCASIONAL NAP.
NEW ART
APPROVED ART
SKIRT TOO SHORT
EAR TOO BIG
ADD FEET
NO
NO
NO
TOO VIOLENT

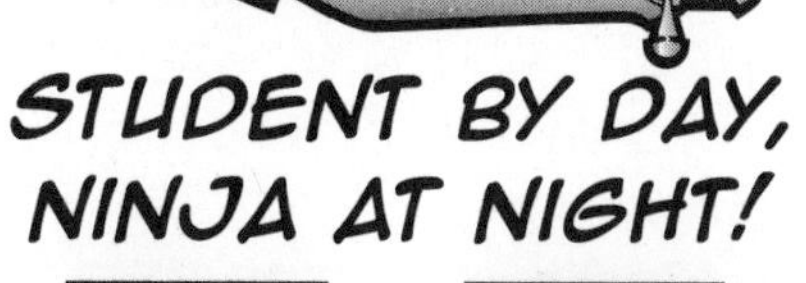

I Was an Eighth-Grade Ninja
Available Now!

My Double-Edged Life
Available Now!

Child of Destiny
Available Now!

The Argon Deception
Available Now!

Secret Alliance
Available Now!

Truth Revealed
Available Soon!

AVAILABLE AT YOUR LOCAL BOOKSTORE!

VOLUMES 6–8 COMING SOON!

ZONDERVAN®

Son of Samson

INCREDIBLE STRENGTH, HEROIC BATTLES, AND HUMOROUS ANTICS!

The Judge of God
Available Now!

The Daughter of Dagon
Available Now!

The Maiden of Thunder
Available Now!

The Raiders of Joppa
Available Now!

The Witch of Endor
Available Now!

The Heroes of God
Available Soon!

AVAILABLE AT YOUR LOCAL BOOKSTORE!

VOLUMES 6–8 COMING SOON!

ZONDERVAN®

FLYING THROUGH TIME TO SAVE THE WORLD!

Pyramid Peril

Available Now!

Turtle Trouble

Available Now!

Berlin Breakout

Available Now!

Tunnel Twist-Up

Available Now!

AVAILABLE AT YOUR LOCAL BOOKSTORE!

VOLUMES 5-8 COMING SOON!

GRAPHIC NOVELS

The Coming Storm
Available Now!

Scions of Josiah
Available Now!

The Prophet's Oracle
Available Now!

Valley of Dry Bones
Available Now!

The Writing on the Wall
Available Now!

Rebuilding Faith
Available Soon!

AVAILABLE AT YOUR LOCAL BOOKSTORE!

VOLUMES 6-8 COMING SOON!